All rights reserved throughout the world.
Published in Great Britain by
World International Publishing Limited.
An Egmont Company,
Egmont House, PO Box 111, Great Ducie Street, Manchester M60 3BL.
Printed in Belgium.
SBN 7235 7271 2.

BOUNTY HUNTER
AND
THE GREENHORN

BOUNTY HUNTER

The circuit flashed. The figure flipped a switch, regarded the image on the screen. He noted the readout.

PATROL WANTED LIST
Location: New Texas . . . Suspect to be captured . . .
Reward 50,000 Credits . . .

*   *   *

Once, New Texas had been a different kind of planet, thought BraveStarr. Before the great Kerium Rush, before the prospectors, and the merchants, and the crooks came.

It had never been a Garden of Eden. It was too hot, too arid ever to have been that. Life had always been hard on New Texas.

Now it was a frontier planet. The riches of Kerium, source of fuel for interstellar spaceships across the galaxy, had attracted both humans and aliens to the hostile planet, like moths to a flame.

Outlaws — along with Kerium crystals — New Texas had in abundance.

But it only had one lawman. He was enough.

*   *   *

Marshal BraveStarr stepped into Main Street, shielding his eyes from the fierce, blood-red sun that hung mercilessly overhead. His footsteps beat their familiar track to Handle Bar's cantina.

At the bar, a customer pleaded with the massive Rigellan who was the owner. Handle Bar was not to be shifted.

"Two Kerium nuggets the sweetwater; ice three nuggets extra," he repeated.

"Okay, okay. Cut the sweetwater, I'll just take the ice," said the customer. "In a tall glass."

"Coming right up."

BraveStarr took his usual place and looked round the bar. There was a crowd of prospectors celebrating a rich strike. He noticed they'd ordered a whole pint of best sweetwater each.

In the corner, seated at a battered upright piano, sat Suggs, Handle Bar's robot pianist.

"Suggs still only playing *Summertime*?" asked BraveStarr.

"His programming's all shot," said Handle Bar, polishing a glass. "I tried putting him on random, but he just improvises."

BraveStarr crossed over to where Suggs sat. "Play it, Suggs," he said.

Suggs looked up. "M-Marshal . . ." he stuttered in a mechanical growl. "B-bad . . . he's coming . . . b-bad . . . it ain't hu-human . . . Hex . . ."

With that, he turned to the keyboards and played a note-perfect version of *Summertime*.

BraveStarr listened thoughtfully and finished his drink. "Thanks Suggs, so long."

Sunlight blazed across his features as he hit the sidewalk again. Thirty/Thirty was waiting for him, a scowl on his face.

"You shouldn't encourage that heap of old junk," the equestroid said. "He gives robots a bad name. Only the other day he was picking up interstellar radio traffic. I tell you, he's long overdue for the meltdown . . ."

BraveStarr's private train of thought was interrupted by Doc Clayton, who called to him as he crossed the street.

"If it's about that annual check-up you mentioned," said BraveStarr, turning to go, "it'll have to wait."

"Can't put it off for forever, Marshal," he insisted. "I'll expect you in my surgery first thing in the morning."

He turned on his heels and went on his way.

Thirty/Thirty stifled a grin. "You sure told him, Marshal. Yup, no question who's the boss there."

Neither he nor BraveStarr saw the sleek, one-man planet-hopper coast in to land at the shuttle pad behind Main Street . . .

*   *   *

The livery stable was about to close for the day when the stranger came in. The Brown Triplets — Khris, Tris and Dan — welcomed the new customer as only Prairie People could, with genuine friendliness, a warm smile, and an eye for how much they could make out of him.

"Welcome, stranger," said Khris.

"A pleasure . . ." said Tris.

". . . to serve you," added Dan. "How we can helpings?"

"First, I need a turbo-mule. Second, you make things to order?" asked the stranger. Then, going on without waiting for an answer, "I need this made. Day after tomorrow."

"Letting me see," said Khris. "Metal, oblong box. Six feets four by two feets wide, one foots deep. Hmm."

"What is it?" said Tris.

The stranger glowered menacingly. "I'm not paying you to ask questions. Just to make the box."

"Make box, certainless sir," said Dan. "No problems."

The stranger took some nuggets from his pocket and counted out a few.

Khris touched the nuggets. "Thank you, sir, that'll do niceness," said Khris. "And, er, you name? For records, you know."

"Kidson. Kit Kidson."

The Brown Triplets watched him leave on the hired turbo-mule. Dan suppressed a shiver.

"Did you seeing those eyes?" he asked. "Maked my blood run cold. Something inhumans about them. Should we tell Marshal?"

"Hear no evil," said Khris.

"See no evil," added Tris.

"Uhuh," said Dan. "Speak no evil. I readings you."

"Sorry about the injection," said Doc Clayton, washing his hands. "Have to run the Kerium allergy test just in case. You'll feel a little groggy for about twenty-four hours."

BraveStarr sat up. The door to the outer office clicked open quietly, and the next moment Kidson stood in the doorway.

"BraveStarr?"

Something in the question made BraveStarr wary, and dulled though his brain was, he managed to utter 'Speed of the Puma!' a fraction of a second before the Neutra-Laser blast hit the wall behind him.

Although weakened, the spirit of the Puma that rose spectrally behind him gave him the necessary speed to reach the street unharmed. He had to think fast. In his present state he'd be a sitting target.

The stratocoach rumbled along Main Street, bound for one of the mining camps with a payroll. Deputy Fuzz was riding shotgun and spotted BraveStarr was in trouble the moment he burst out of Doc Clayton's door.

Grabbing the reins he swung the coach across the street.

"Hop aboard!" he yelled. Deputy Fuzz's multirope coiled round BraveStarr's waist and pulled him on the speeding vehicle.

The street was empty by the time Kidson made the boardwalk. A cold light came into his eyes, a look of ruthless determination. He swung into the saddle of his turbo-mule. It was time to seek out his ally . . . Tex Hex.

*   *   *

When he was sure there was no pursuit, Deputy Fuzz pulled the stratocoach to a halt. Stepping down he went to check on BraveStarr.

"You okay?"

"Weak," said BraveStarr, shaking his head to try and clear it. He took a deep breath. "Thanks, Deputy, I reckon I owe you for that. Some guy with real mean eyes had the drop on me."

"Mean eyes, huh?" asked Deputy Fuzz thoughtfully. "Seeming to me I heard some talks of him amongst the Prairie Peoples at livery stable. Come in last night. Name of Kidson. Kit Kidson. You knowing him?"

"I've heard of him," said BraveStarr. "Bounty hunter out of Cygnus Five. Can't figure why he's after me, though."

The image of Suggs swam into BraveStarr's mind. "I think I've got it figured," he said. "I'd better call Thirty/Thirty on the Starrtalker. I reckon we can expect company soon. It won't take Kidson long to pick up my trail."

It was a short wait.

"They told me you were the best, Kidson," Tex Hex was complaining.

Kidson eyed him coldly. "I am. You wanna try me, Hex?"

Vipra interrupted. "Quit jawing you two. We came to do a job remember. We've got a fix on him now. Kidson will take BraveStarr, we'll handle the equestroid. Split up."

They arrived in time to see the stratocoach throwing up a trail of dust as it disappeared over the plain. Despite his protests, Deputy Fuzz had taken the payroll to safety, after Thirty/Thirty had arrived.

Tex Hex put his Hexmaker to work. As they closed on Thirty/Thirty and found the range, he dug into his bandolier and selected one of his Hexloads. The air crackled with freeze rays, and then the Hexload burst over Thirty/Thirty's hideout.

Immediately the rocks transformed into a stone cage from which the courageous equestroid could find no escape. Tex Hex and Vipra closed in.

Meanwhile, BraveStarr and Kidson were playing a deadly game of hide-and-seek. It ended when the bounty hunter got the drop on his prey from behind.

"Nice and easy now, BraveStarr," said Kidson. "And keep that hand away from the Neutra-Laser. No tricks."

BraveStarr let his Neutra-Laser fall. This was it: Kidson had him cold.

"Makes no difference to me if you come quietly or not. Reward's the same," said Kidson, coming round to face BraveStarr. "If there's one thing I can't stand it's an android slaver, like you. Speaking *personally* I don't hold with the idea that the only good android is a tame android!"

As he spoke, Kidson pulled open a flap in his shirt and made an adjustment to his control panel.

BraveStarr looked down the barrel of the Neutra-Laser and remained ice-cool. "I never knew an android to make a mistake before on an electronic i.d."

Kidson's eyes narrowed. "I'm not programmed to make mistakes, mister." The Neutra-Laser hovered before BraveStarr's face.

"Unless someone's been tampering with the database, feeding in false information," observed BraveStarr. "Check it out, my android friend."

*   *   *

Thirty/Thirty was making a bold stand. Trapped and unable to manoeuvre for position, he was doing his best to hold off Tex Hex and Vipra as they advanced from opposite directions.

Tex Hex grinned evilly as he launched another Hexload at the beleaguered equestroid. "This is where Thirty/Thirty becomes Zero/Zero," he hissed, and moved in to deliver the final blow.

The rock above him vaporized into a million pieces. Hex looked round in amazement to see Kidson with his Neutra-Laser levelled at him.

"That's far enough," said Kidson. "Violation of computer records is a serious crime, mister."

BraveStarr joined him. "It was a neat ploy to falsify a Priority Arrest Order for me, Tex Hex," said the lawman, "but my friend Kidson doesn't take to being lied to."

Tex Hex didn't wait a second longer. Firing his Hexmaker, he released a cloud of sleep gas. Kidson and BraveStarr were fast enough to throw themselves clear, but by the time the danger was passed Tex Hex and Vipra were long gone.

Thirty/Thirty was mighty glad to see a friendly face.

"About time the cavalry arrived," he said from inside his stone cage, "before I had to do my impression of Thirty/Thirty's last stand."

Summoning the 'Strength of the Bear!' BraveStarr lifted the huge rocks and freed his companion. As they parted company from Kidson, the android paused to say his farewells.

"Reckon I'll be heading off-planet now, BraveStarr," said Kidson, "but I'll be back. Only next time I'll come looking for the right target."

THE GREENHORN

BraveStarr and Thirty/Thirty stood at the checkout terminal watching the passengers as they filed out of the space-pod. They looked like the usual newcomers to New Texas . . . a group of prospectors hoping to strike it rich in the Kerium mines, a trader or two, a couple of shifty types who had trouble written all over them and the odd drifter.

"That's him," said BraveStarr, as he noticed a tall, fresh-faced young man from Earth.

"Yep, pardner," Thirty/Thirty agreed gloomily. "What's the point of sending a greenhorn rookie marshal out here?"

"It's only for a few days," grinned BraveStarr. "Give the boy a chance."

"Your first chance is your last chance when some raygun totin' ugly fires first and asks questions later," Thirty/Thirty grumbled.

The young man walked over and stood to attention, saluting the Marshal.

"Trainee Marshal 5689 reporting from the Galactic Marshal Academy for one week of active duty to preserve law and order on New Texas, sir."

"Skip the formalities, son," smiled BraveStarr. "Gimme your luggage."

The young man looked shocked and pointed to Thirty/Thirty. "With respect, sir, shouldn't the equestroid be made to carry the luggage?"

"This equestroid *respectfully* declines," said Thirty/Thirty coolly. "Carry your own bags, sunshine."

"What's your name?" asked BraveStarr, interrupting diplomatically.

"Wally K. Parrot," came the reply.

"Parrot?" asked Thirty/Thirty gleefully.

"Parrot!" repeated the newcomer.

"Hee-hee. You sure sound like one," wheezed Thirty/Thirty. Then noting the look of annoyance he continued, "It's a joke. Parrot, repeating things you see like a . . .like a . . .Aw, shucks. No offence, boy."

"Listen, equestroid, and listen good," snapped the young man, "failure to address a lawman by his proper title is an offence under Statute 674 and can lead to a fine of two thousand nuggets. Understand?"

"Yes, Trainee Marshal 5689," said Thirty/Thirty meekly, and added under his breath, "I understand . . . *boy!*"

BraveStarr said nothing, but he was worried. New Texas wasn't the kind of a place for a greenhorn lawman full of his own importance.

*   *   *

The blood-red sun hung like a wound in the grey sky as the thunder rumbled and clouds of dust started to rise and swirl round the plains of The Badlands.

Tex Hex stood on top of the plateau of rock and stared up at the sky. Even the most evil man on New Texas felt himself dwarfed and almost fearful as the rocks echoed the booming noise and the swirling clouds formed into a gigantic, solid shape.

The sun was obscured from sight and the land was bathed in an eerie shadow. For a few moments the evil spirit of Stampede, the mighty broncosaur hung in the sky.

Tex Hex threw back his head and cackled in delight as the strange shape gradually faded back into nothingness.

The mystical, menacing appearance of Stampede was a sign to Tex telling him of new ways to create chaos. He now knew his plans. He knew the place where he would defeat BraveStarr once and for all . . .

* * *

In the main street of Fort Kerium the argument was getting very heated. Three tough looking characters, bear-like in size and appearance, towered above a nervous six-armed prospector from the Orfen Galaxy. A wagon of Kerium was nearby.

"Kerium our that's," growled one of the bear men.

"What's he saying, sir?" The Trainee Marshal fired the question at BraveStarr as they crossed the street.

"They're the Backtalk Boys from Betelgeuse," said BraveStarr, watching the quarrel from the corner of his eye. "Always speak backwards when they use our language."

"Those guys are liable to get into a fight," said the young man.

"Yep," agreed BraveStarr.

"We could take 'em in and slap a 735 order on them," protested the trainee. "Aren't you going to do anything?"

"Nope!" replied BraveStarr, heading towards Handle Bar's cantina.

"Us to back it give," demanded one of the Backtalk Boys. He pointed a huge finger at the small prospector. "Angry getting I'm."

"Now let's not be hasty, fellas," begged the prospector.

"Fight gonna you," snarled a Backtalk Boy.

"Hold it right there!" commanded Trainee Marshal Parrot, as he calmly walked towards the argument. "There'll be no fighting while I'm around."

"Sonny, off clear," boomed the largest Backtalk Boy. He reached forward and grabbed the youngster and lifted him up in the air.

Suddenly, BraveStarr was among them. Calling 'Strength of the Bear', BraveStarr sprang into action, overpowering the six-armed prospector. He took from him a tiny pistol which had been pointing at Trainee Marshal Parrot.

"Okay, Backtalk Boys," grinned BraveStarr. "Take your Kerium. I'm taking this skunk in for stealing."

With a satisfied grunt, the Boys' leader dropped the rookie lawman into the dust. The trio walked to the cantina, grinning and laughing.

"BraveStarr around you see," they called.

"Don't never go looking for trouble, Trainee Marshal 5689," said Thirty/Thirty, ambling up the street. "Bide your time and see what happens. That's what the Marshal does."

"The little guy had that pistol in his hand from the start," said BraveStarr. "I could see it glinting in the sun. When your back was turned he had the drop on you. He would have pinned the blame on the Backtalk Boys."

"I . . . I see," said Parrot. He picked himself up and dusted himself down. "But those crazy bears still assaulted an officer. They should be charged for that."

"Okay," said BraveStarr. "Go tell 'em, if that's how you feel."

"Well . . . er," Parrot hesitated, "maybe I'll let them off . . . just this once!"

*   *   *

Some hours later Deputy Fuzz came racing into the jail.

"Tex Hex has stealing stratocoach from Main Street and drive out of town," he gasped, before realizing that BraveStarr was not there. In the Marshal's place was Trainee Marshal Parrot. He was wearing full uniform, including hat.

"Sorry," apologised Deputy Fuzz. "Didn't knowing was only you."

"I take full responsibility while the Marshal isn't here," said the trainee, proudly. "I'll take Thirty/Thirty and ride out after Tex Hex."

"But . . . but . . . but . . ."

"No buts, Deputy. I'm on my way."

Moments later Marshal BraveStarr returned from rounding up some robocattle rustlers. On hearing Fuzz's news he sprang into action. Summoning 'Speed of the Puma', the lawman raced out of town, following the trail of the stratocoach.

Before long he could see the coach and its pursuers far across an arid plain that rose sharply into a wall of rock. Tex Hex knew every inch of the area that bordered on The Badlands. He could have taken a much shorter, quicker way. Why had he decided to cut round the plain that doubled back to the rocks? It was as if Tex Hex *wanted* to be followed.

BraveStarr summoned the 'Eyes of the Hawk'. As the spectral shape of the bird rose behind him, BraveStarr turned his attention on the outcrop of rock. There was a narrow pass going through it. Perched high on the sides of the rock face were a whole army of Tex Hex's villainous associates. Hex had planned an ambush and the Trainee Marshal and Thirty/Thirty were heading towards it.

The New Texas lawman looked towards the solid rock face that flanked the pass. There may be just enough time using the puma's speed . . .

* * *

Thirty/Thirty had been grumbling all the way. When the first hail of rays exploded round his hooves, the equestroid decided that he really did have something to complain about.

At lightning speed, Thirty/Thirty transformed to humanoid stance and his lever-action freeze rifle was blasting round him.

As luck had it, there was a large boulder nearby and the equestroid and the Trainee Marshal were able to throw themselves behind it to find cover.

"Can't hold out here for ever," observed Thirty/Thirty. "We've walked straight into an ambush. Tex Hex and his cronies have got us where they want us."

"Suppose I give myself up," suggested the young lawman. "Maybe Tex Hex would let you go. It's my fault this happened."

"No way, Trainee Marshal 5689," grinned Thirty/Thirty. "You and me'll see this out together."

The outlaws were moving nearer and nearer, secure in their strength of numbers and in the protection that the rock afforded.

Suddenly there was a cry of dismay from Tex Hex. A landslide of rocks was tumbling down from the hillside. Confusion and chaos set in amongst the crowd of cowards. The tunnels made by the Prairie People were welcome retreats for many of them.

"That evens things out, Tex Hex," came a commanding voice from the summit of the rock face.

"BraveStarr!" cried Tex Hex, beside himself with fury. "B-but I thought . . ." The outlaw looked in amazement at the figure in the Marshal's outfit at the foot of the valley and the figure of BraveStarr moving down the cliff towards him. He didn't stay to work things out but decided that retreating into one of the tunnels was the safest course of action.

"Yeehaa!" cried Thirty/Thirty, as the last of the outlaws scurried from the scene. "Nice work, Marshal."

Using the 'Strength of the Bear', BraveStarr had moved the boulders and started the landslide.

"Guess I owe you all an apology," admitted the Trainee Marshal. "Thought being out in the real world was just like being at the training academy."

"Don't worry about it, son," smiled BraveStarr. "We've all got to learn sometime. And the lawman's got a mighty lot to learn. But there is one job I'd like you to handle on your own. A tough task, but . . ."

"I can do it, sir. I know I can," interrupted the youngster.

"Well then, get across to the Dry Falls Kerium mine. I want you to make sure there's no trouble going on there."

"Yes, sir," said the would-be lawman, eager to be given a responsible, important job to do.

"But, Marshal," said Thirty/Thirty, as Trainee Marshal 5689 walked away, "the Dry Falls mine hasn't been used for years. Ain't nothin' going to be happening over there."

"Then our young friend should have it nice and easy for a while," grinned Marshal BraveStarr. "And so should we, pardner."